TIME
TELLS

TIME TELLS

STEVE FOPPIANO

TATE PUBLISHING
AND ENTERPRISES, LLC

Published by Tate Publishing & Enterprises, LLC
127 E. Trade Center Terrace | Mustang, Oklahoma 73064 USA
1.888.361.9473 | www.tatepublishing.com

Tate Publishing is committed to excellence in the publishing industry. The company reflects the philosophy established by the founders, based on Psalm 68:11,
"The Lord gave the word and great was the company of those who published it."

Book design copyright © 2014 by Tate Publishing, LLC. All rights reserved.
Cover design by Rtor Maghuyop
Interior design by Mary Jean Archival

Published in the United States of America

ISBN: 978-1-63367-887-3
1. Fiction / Christian / General
2. Fiction / Christian / Historical
14.09.04

The Glass of Water

Walter's story:

Let me introduce myself. My name is Walter Storys. I have a story to tell, and even though it may seem unbelievable, it really happened. I won't get offended if you simply read this tale for entertainment and then call me crazy. What I'm getting ready to tell you happened to me and I have a hard time believing it. But whether you're going to believe it or not, tie your shoes, put on your hat, and let's go on this little journey together.

To begin with, let me tell you a little bit about myself. As long as I can remember, I would have trouble falling asleep at night. Sleep for me would be like walking uphill backward. I would always get to the top but only after much work. Now that I'm some older, I've become accustomed to this uphill battle. I play the "what if" game up in the thinkin' part of my brain. Here's how it plays for me: "Would I be happier if I was smarter?" or "Would I be more content if I was one of the doctors who cured cancer?" I contemplated many different things when most of America is asleep. If you could think it, I probably already thunk it.

It was during one of these late nights that my thinkin' got interrupted, invaded may be a better word for it. Sometimes, my thinkin' runs to the silly side, and tonight, I was all over on that side. I was doing animal combinations in my head. You know what I mean, don't you? I was giving monkeys the ears of an elephant or big ole lions some penguin's feet and watching them roar and chase their food. Sometimes, I can really make myself laugh. But what happened next was no laughing matter. As my mind was thinkin', my eyes were fixed on a clock I have in my bedroom. My eyes were watching the hands circling around the face of the clock when all of a sudden, the clock began to transform itself into a face, an actual face. Yea, eyes, nose, the whole works! Here I am now, wide awake, watching something happen that to the normal mind would seem like a miracle or crazy. I told myself, "This can't really be happening." I went to the kitchen and got a glass of water and brought it with me and set it on my nightstand. Mind you, I would not even look at the wall where my clock was hangin'. I thought I was going crazy.

I lay back down, drank some water, and then looked right at that silly ole clock. Well, what would you do? Would you run away? Come back and trash that clock? Or do what I did, come back and see what ole Mr. Clock had to say?

Oh boy, did that clock had something to say, too! That ole clock started talking and, as a matter of fact, is still talking to this day. I'm tryin' to think back how long this has been going on, probably about nine and a half years. Figuring I get about two haircuts a year, this miracle started about eighteen haircuts ago. A couple of years ago, the winter was colder then usual so I made myself miss my winter haircut to help keep my head warm. So yea, that ole clock started telling me things about nine and a half years ago. You have to excuse me, sometimes I get to rambling about something or other, but I always come back to the important stuff.

They say that clocks tell time, but I'm here to tell ya that they do a lot more than that. This here clock took me on a journey. The hands of that clock scooped me up and we went whooshing to another time. Mind you, I can't explain how any of this happened, I just know that it did. I also don't know how an airplane flies or a big ole ship floats, but I've been on both and can testify that they both work.

Mr. Clock took me to a place and time that I can only describe as "the beginning." There's many things that go without saying…but not this. Before I continue, I have to tell ya that I've always believed in God, the devil, and all the stories the Bible tells us. If you don't, then that's on you. But I just can't wrap my mind around the complexity of humans, the way the world works, and not believe in God. And then I look at all the evil in the world and can see plainly the devil's hand on our lives.

I've read the story in Genesis about when God created us and I've always believed it. Boy, let me tell you, now I know it to be true. Before my mind believed, now my heart knows it!

Mr. Clock introduced me to the one and only Adam. If you had time, you could probably sit down and write about a thousand questions to ask him. But I'm a simple man, and all the questions you might have now, I couldn't think of to ask him. All I could do was stare. Rude as I knew it to be, I could not take my eyes off him. I'm not afraid to say that pink is my favorite color or to express an interest in flowers. Yet I've never called another man beautiful until now! Adam was beautiful and amazing to look at.

In order for that last statement to sound good to *myself,* I must explain it this way: the Adam that I shook hands with was the Adam that was made in God's own image. The Adam I shook hands with was the Adam before the devil tricked him. And the Adam I shook hands with was the Adam that still had Eve in him. God hadn't yet taken

Eve out of him. So like I said, Adam was beautiful and I was drawn to him.

He talked and I listened. Heck, what did I have to contribute? I could tell him about airplanes, pizza, and televisions. But I was in a place now where flavors exploded in your mouth, where colors were actually alive, and where you could tickle a grizzly—and hear him laugh. So I just listened.

He told me that monkeys tell the funniest jokes, at least they think so. That eagles are the best at playing tag and dogs have absolutely no sense of humor. He also said that when snakes play, they do not play fair.

I was there to listen. I knew that. Some things you just know. In my world, you know that gravity works. You know that we can't breathe under water. We also know that joy is a good thing and we want as much as we can get. I also knew that I did not bring myself to this place. I knew that I was here for a reason. And I knew that I was here to listen. I listened!

Adam told me of his experiences of naming each animal, of how they responded with such great joy. All of a sudden, he turned silent. In his silence, I became aware of my surroundings. There was light everywhere. I could see under the leaves and behind the trees, nothing was hidden or even cast a shadow. I could see inside the animals, inside the trees, and even inside the ground. Everywhere I could see, there it was: *light*.

Everything seemed so alive. Even the noise that was there, it wasn't random. Each blade of grass, each animal, each color played an instrument. All the music from this garden blended together into one masterpiece. And I listened.

The funny thing was that there was so much to listen to. When Adam spoke, he said a lot. But when he was silent, much more was said. This could be just me, but I think when words are used to communicate there is so much that can't be translated into our vocabulary that whole chapters are left unsaid.

This is where my words are gonna fall a bit short. I'm gonna try and explain the unexplainable. I know what you're thinkin', "That's just crazy, these must be the words of a madman." All I can say is you just may be right. Let go and hang on 'cause here we go.

While I was on this journey with ole Mr. Clock, as I was experiencing the events in the beginning, there was absolutely no doubt that everything around me was completely and totally real. When Adam's eyes and mine locked onto each other, there was a joining of souls that was pure and without anything corrupt. I can almost still feel the ground that I walked on in that far-off place.

Let me ask you, do you have a favorite teacher? Or do you remember that first person you fell in love with? How about your favorite food, can you describe it? Mine is cheesecake, it is sweet and its flavor explodes in my mouth. I can pick it out of any other dessert. I still remember the encouragement my English teacher showered me with. I remember the red freckles on Sandy's fifth grade face, and I remember cheesecake. As much as I love these memories and know them to be true, they are just a fraction of the actual experiences. Here's the thing, of all these memories that I know and have personally experienced, while I was "away," all my Sandy, cheesecake, and teacher memories seemed vague and unreal. On the other hand, there are always two hands, while I'm here and writing these experiences, my time with Adam and ole Mr. Clock are the dreamy ones.

Can you imagine what it felt like for me when I woke up that next morning? There I was with last night's experiences still fresh in my mind, but *fading*. Woke up may not be the exact term I should use, landed may be more appropriate. Either way, I came to myself right there in my room. I looked over at my nightstand, and there it was, my half-drank glass of water. That to me was enough evidence of last night's encounter.

What I'm about to say I know just about everyone can relate to. Those who can't may be not totally honest or may not fully understand my meaning. Let me try and explain. Have you ever been doing something or going somewhere and you had a sudden feeling to stop or change direction?

Did a voice in your head tell you something? I'm not talking about an actual voice that anyone else can hear or a voice to have a conversation with. It's like a feeling and a thought all rolled up into one.

There was a time I was driving home along a river road and I was coming up to a blind curve. Whatever you want to call it, let's say it was a voice in my head, "it" convinced me to slow down. If I had not slowed down, the car that was driving way to fast and running into my lane would have certainly hit me and very possibly killed me. It was that very same voice that told me two little words as I was gazing upon that glass of half-drank water. Those two words have carried me from then to now. Those words were "just believe."

C an you believe that two little words could be so significant in changing a man's life? Even if you just think about it a little, the answer has to be yes. The normal person has to believe that they will finish what they start. People go to college believing they will graduate. They don't pay all that money believing they will drop out before they finish. The normal person who goes to college believes they will graduate and then work in their field of study. And for the most part, it happens. Their lives have been changed, dramatically changed. Just like mine was when I believed the chain of events that took place in my life.

I have to go back and tell ya a bit more of what happened on my first trip and about the personalities that I came in contact with. I say personalities due to the fact they were not human, but you could sure hold conversations with them. Remember that ole clock that whooshed me away back in the beginning of this story? Well, the two hands that picked me up did most all the talkin'. Their names were Tick and Tock.

These two are not major characters in this story. But I do have to spend a little time in talkin' about them. I have to make you understand that Tick and Tock are not comedians and they did not try to make me laugh, they told no jokes, but there were times when I was laughing so hard that you could probably call it exercise. Have you ever laughed so hard your stomach got a workout? Well, there were, it seemed, whole days I lived there. The beauty of it was they understood and did not get offended. At all!

They sure know how to have fun. Tick was the minute hand, he did all the talkin'. Tock was the second hand and he did the majority of the tickin'. In other words, he kept the time. He would let us know when it was time to go or if we could stay a little longer. Tock could talk too; he just talked so fast I couldn't understand a word he said. So Tick talked for both of them. Whatever Tick said, Tock was in complete agreement. There was never an argument or a time of disagreement.

It was amusing and even funny to watch their interactions. When Tick talked and explained some deep mystery to me, I would notice Tock's expression and it said something like this, "That's exactly what I was going to say and how I was going to say it!" And that would happen with both of them all the time! They sure made me laugh.

Enough about Tick and Tock for now. As amusing and entertaining as they are, we must continue the story. The story for now is about the place where I met Adam. Let's call it The Garden. Backing up just a little, I must say that the significance of a clock being my guide was not lost on me. Every place I went, the specific time I was there had everything to do with this excursion. "When" I was was just as important as "where" I was.

This time I was in The Garden after everything was made, but before any of the work was delegated. Today was the Seventh Day. It was the day of celebration. It was the day of rest. It was the day God ceased from His work. It was the day of blessing.

Tick was tellin' me a little about what today was all about. But while he was doing all the talkin', I felt like a little puppy on a leash that just wanted to run wild. Just let me go so I could get to playin'. That's what I was thinkin', but what I was doing was listenin'. Everything that I saw and everything that was said made perfect sense. Even though the things that I witnessed were contrary to anything I've ever experienced before.

For example, like I said before, bears are ticklish and giggled rather silly. But even more than that, wolves and lambs laid together, gazelles and cheetahs rested head to head, and bats and bugs were on the same team. There was a connectedness in this Garden that brought everything together.

I have come from a place and time where evil things dwell, but back here, they haven't been born yet. Fear, jealousy, greed, hate, just to name a few, have not invaded our hearts yet. I can admit that I know about those feelings pretty good, maybe too good. So that being said, I can also recognize when they are absent. Well, all those emotions and much more, everything that could or would cause grief was absent in The Garden. It was a place of newness. If I got to stay here forever, it would not be long enough.

How do you explain color to someone who can't see? Or a caress to someone with no ability to feel a touch. There are new and different colors here. I didn't only see them, I heard them, tasted them, and even smelled them! The only way I have to describe them is to tell you their names and hope your imagination will take over. Think about this first: when you see the color, you also taste it and feel it. Or when you taste it, you also see it and feel it. It is a complete experience. Oh, how I wish you could come with me! One day, one day maybe!

Meanwhile, come with me in this story. If you can just experience in part what I did, you will be inspired to come all the way. There is a way, and it is simple. But I will talk about that at a later time.

But for now, let me tell you about the color of Joy. There was an explosion in me when Joy touched my heart. It was brand-new to me, something I have never experienced before or since. I don't think I can explain it visually, but I hope I can explain it to you by how it made me feel. To use the words *happy*, *glad*, or even *joyful* would just begin to touch the color of Joy. All those words are true, but they are not enough. One thing I've always wanted to do was fly like Superman. Everybody knows that's impossible, that's never happenin', that's just plain crazy. But still, I would love to soar through the clouds freestyle, dodging birds and mountains. If you could imagine what that would be like, then you could begin to see shades of Joy!

Let me see if I can explain the problem I'm having now. Do you know when someone goes on vacation, they pick out the highlights or the best parts to tell you? They may either tell you the best of the best or just leave out the not so good parts. Well, everything that I experienced, saw, felt, heard, or tasted is well worth talkin' about. The problem is that there just isn't enough time or paper to tell ya'll everything. Please realize that whatever I'm tellin' ya is just a very tiny part of what I experienced. But if this tale starts you to thinkin' about a better place and how great it is, then the joy in my heart will be complete.

There's another color I want to talk a little about before we move on. It's going to be a little more difficult to describe than Joy but just as true and inspiring.

Some people are smart and do things that we call wise. Some people give us advice that we call wise and it even helps us through difficult situations. We call a person that seems so smart a man of wisdom. I would not dare to argue with anyone with those kind of smarts. I'm just a simple man. But pause and reflect on this: the color of Wisdom has nothing to do with how we do business in this society. The color Wisdom does not have anything to do with information. It has nothing to do with sequential events that make sense in a logical way. The color Wisdom is not an impulsive act. To experience Wisdom, to run with her, and to taste her, you must jump into her river. The water in "that" river is crying out for you to breathe her in. She does not belong on the outside of your body pushing you through the current. You must breathe her in. It does not make any sense, because it just may seem like you will drown and your purpose will end. But it will be at that time when you open your mouth to breath, Wisdom will come in like a flood and you will see *purpose*.

For a brief moment, I experienced purpose. I knew the purpose of Wisdom, of Joy, of even The Garden. I new the purpose of Color itself. When I experienced Wisdom, it was like touching the very hand of the one who made everything. When I did that, I understood more than I cared to. Just to make things clear, in order to come back here, I had to get out of that river. There are moments of clarity now when I can experience Wisdom, but only in part. But there are times now when Wisdom will tell me to smile at someone. I will, because I also am shown the purpose of that smile, where it is meant to go and what it is meant to do. The purpose of Wisdom always promotes life.

Well, Tick is talkin' right now and he's tellin' me that Tock is tellin' us to move on to the next phase of this story. The funny thing is up until Tick started tellin' me that Tock said it was time to go, I had forgotten that Tick and Tock were right beside me. There they were, even holding my hands, and I had totally forgotten about them. Time had moved forward even though I went backward. The more I think about it, the dizzier I get.

I came to myself in my bedroom hearing the tick-tock of this now lifeless clock hanging on my wall. The truest thing I can tell you about that moment was I was at a loss. I didn't know if I was awake or asleep. Had I died and left my body? Or was I alive but lost my mind? Although my mind was going down a road where it seemed I had lost the steering wheel, there was another force in my heart that told me everything is going to be all right.

If anyone came up to me and told me even half the things that happened to me, I would be backstepping with my feet and dialing for the men in white jackets. So I knew what I went through sounded crazy, but I also knew I wasn't crazy. I may be a simple man, but I wasn't a stupid one. The fact was that I didn't know anyone well enough to tell this to without doing what I would do in the same situation, which was call for the men in white jackets. I just did what I thought any normal red-blooded person would do, I pondered it in my heart and hoped it would go away over time.

This is the pause and reflect time. I'm gonna be askin' a question that will probably come around the corner a few times in this story. What would you do in this situation if you were me? Not "What would *you* do?"

The way I saw it, I could tell one of my few friends what happened and probably lose my friendship with him. Or I could do what I did and just bury it in my heart. As you can probably guess, even though I buried it, it didn't stay there for long.

3

I woke up rested even though the sleep I slept was no sleep at all. I was alert and awake the whole day, but if you asked me to spell my name, I don't think I coulda put two letters together to make any sense. I walked around in a weird fog all day. Almost everybody I ran into, even people I didn't know, were askin' me the same question. It was like they knew what happened to me, but they could not have known. For example, a person in the check-out line gave me a weird look and asked me if I "could believe it?" I could feel my jaw drop open and then he pointed to the newspaper and made a comment I don't remember. Then a friend called me on the phone and said the same thing, "Could I believe it?" Then there was something said about a relative winning the lottery. This kinda thing happened too many times that day to call it a coincidence.

I could not ignore the obvious. First, that little voice in my head telling me to "just believe." Then all these people asking me that very same thing: "Do I believe?" If you woulda asked me which was more strange, what happened to me after I went to bed or what happened after I got up, I coulda flipped a coin to give you a right answer. I was too scared to answer my own question of "Was I going crazy or was I already there?"

That next night brought me to the next day in my "Garden" adventure. I'm sure a lot happened in between my garden adventures. I just wasn't there for them. When I went to bed that night, good ole Tick and Tock whooshed me away again to that very same Garden. Only this time, it wasn't the day of rest, it was a day of activity.

Before we arrived in the Garden, my new friends told me a little of what to expect. There would be someone new there to greet us. Even though I would be meeting her for the first time, I would recognize her. Tick was talkin', but my brain could not take in all he was tellin' me. So my thought was to chew on it awhile until it made sense. I mean, come on, I would recognize someone I never met before?

We, or should I say he (Tick), talked for a bit as we strolled to my new destination. Tick tried to prepare me for the "time" we were about to enter into. Think about it for a minute. Here I was, an ordinary man, on my way to over the hill, walkin' hand and hand with two hands of a clock hangin' from my wall on my way to The Garden to see the Adam of the Bible! Prepare me for what? Every time I turned around, stuff popped out to strike me as miraculous. Most of the stuff there I couldn't begin to explain. I can only tell ya the things I experienced with words that fall way short of the actual place and time. Let me put it this way: if you think you can imagine what I'm tryin' to explain to you, you are a million miles away from it. No mind can begin to come up to the beauty there. If crazy was where I was headin', then I guess there are worse places to be.

Well, go figure! As I entered into my destination, there was Adam. He was there with open arms to introduce me to his new wife: Eve. Tick was right, I sure did recognize her and she me too. She was beautiful. She was just like Adam to look at, but she was all female. I was drawn to her the same way I was drawn to Adam. I didn't mention this before because it didn't seem important. But now, it seems I must mention it. They were both naked. It was not weird or unnatural though! The weird part is that it wasn't weird. They were complete in their attire. There was no shame or embarrassment, no pride or false pride, just joy and love.

As much as the two were alike, they were also different and separate individuals. In the obvious ways, they were almost twins. They looked the same, they had the same mannerisms, and where one went, the other was right there alongside. They never did anything apart. They were truly like a king and queen who knew their place.

For the short amount of time I was with Adam, I got to know his ways fairly well. He had a way about him that was both motherly and fatherly. Now, if you can understand this, *they* were no different than he *was*. The qualities he had as Adam they now shared as Adam and Eve. She was excitable in a way that was filled with joy and newness. He was less impulsive and more contemplative. They would always get to the same place, she would just arrive first. He would begin a sentence, she would finish it. It was beautiful to watch them work together. It would be something like a great painter painting a picture equally well with both hands at the same time.

And work they did. I have never seen so much accomplished in such little time with everything in The Garden working together. Every tree, every bush, every blade of grass had purpose in The Garden. Every animal, every bird, and every insect had a job to do.

The work you or I may do in our garden is way different then the work that went on in The Garden. We dig, plant, prune, water, spray for bugs, and as a rule get pretty dirty. In this place, in this Garden, in this protected place, things work a little different. There are no shovels, no pruning sheers, or even water hoses. There is dirt, but even the dirt is not dirty. You could eat off the ground if the opportunity arose.

This is how it worked. Adam knew the condition of each tree, each piece of fruit, and each animal. In this special place, the animals did the work. Even the bugs all worked together. It is commonly known that bees work hard in nature to pollinate flowers and produce honey. Can you imagine everything, all animals, even bugs, and all that is rooted in the ground workin' together? The thing that is missing in today's bees was not missing in anything in The Garden. The Joy, Excitement, and Playfulness was in every living thing in The Garden. There was never a distraction from doing their assigned tasks. Doing their tasks was what they all had fun doing.

Have I mentioned yet how beautiful it was there? Not just the beauty that I experienced with my senses. If you've ever watched an artist put together a masterpiece or an orchestra play a piece when each instrument had significance and a purpose. Each brush stroke or each note taking you on a journey that led you to a place of beauty in the craftsmanship alone.

Reflecting back on all I heard there, in all the words and expressions that were said there, there was one word that was never said—or even thought. No one or nothing, not an animal or even a blade of grass ever told Adam "no."

Can you imagine all the arguments or fights that would not take place in today's world if we would remove that word from our vocabulary? Well, maybe I'm thinkin' on the silly side again.

B am! It was evening, now it's morning and a new day. The clocks were back to normal. Tick took me back to my bed and now was just tickin' and not talkin'. Tock was back to what he always did: keepin' time. Now I was as hungry as a skeleton.

There was something going on that had me totally confused. Don't laugh. I mean something other than the obvious insanity that has already played out. If I were asked to describe it in one word, that word would be *change*. I was changing. I don't quite know into what yet, but my thought was that it's going to be a good thing.

You could look at me and probably not see anything different. Let's see if I can put it in a way we both can understand: If I were a house, you would look at my outside and see that all would be as it was, no change. The color, landscape, and all the outside fixins would be untouched. But if you were to walk through the inside, the old floor plan and the new one would be totally different.

Now mind you, I know where it was done, but I surely don't know how. I suspect I never will, and I'm totally okay with that. I am a little curious, but it's not one of those things that drive ya crazy if you don't know.

I'm mostly a coffee and toast man for breakfast, but this morning, I scrambled up about four eggs to go along with today's plans. These plans ain't any plans I conjured up on my own, but I knew I had a choice in them and that they were not for my harm.

Today, I have the luxury of lookin' back and seeing how everything came together. At the time, I felt totally unprepared for what was to come. Lookin' back now, I see I had everything that was needed. Back, when I first was taken to The Garden to meet Adam, he planted something in me that grew like a well-watered seed. What it was, I didn't know, but I sure felt it growin' in me.

I'm in a place now where I'm kinda set in my ways. But my ways were a-changing. Me and my neighbor had this little game we played where his dog would dig under our fence and get in my yard. I would then call him up and leave a nasty message on his recorder, and well, you could guess the rest. This morning, when I saw his dog in my backyard,

I had a sudden inspiration. I went to the pet store and bought a sack of dog food and a dog bowl. I proceeded to cut a hole in our fence for his dog to come through. I made it nice and pretty, and I gave Jake, their dog, permission to come in my yard. I even made a sign that said "Welcome" to put up for all to see.

I left a message on my neighbor's voice mail that was quite different then all the other messages. I really surprised myself in a good way. Ya know, being friendly felt a whole lot better than feelin' angry all the time. Besides, when I looked at Jake in my yard or thought of my next-door neighbor, these are actual living beings, I could not bring myself to be mean or get angry at them anymore for messin' up a yard that felt on pain. I don't know why I never saw it that way before. Who is this new person that came to live in my house?

If you haven't figured it out yet, I'm retired and so I have no obligation to any employer or any fixed work schedule. That doesn't mean I have nothing to do all day. I stay plenty busy. I take great pride in my yard. I enjoy doing yard work so much that I help out around the neighborhood for people who are less healthy than me. I have always been healthy, even now being on the other side of the hill. I volunteer at the soup kitchen once a week and even look for and collect donations at different stores to help feed more people. I'm learning there are a lot of hungry people out there. I also help out at my local church, mostly just 'cause I'm available.

I said all that to say this: I stay busy, I don't just sit at home and twiddle my thumbs. The next couple of nights were uneventful if you were just lookin' at my nightly wanderings. But that does not mean peculiar things weren't happening. Don't get me wrong, dogs still barked, birds flew, and life went on normally. But there was a feelin' in me that was growin'. It was both a concern for people around me and also a sadness that was way bigger than me. Little did I know I would soon find out what it all meant.

Tick and Tock came back to me again. After a couple of nights without my timekeepers to talk with, I thought maybe "Time" had stood still for a while. Not so. But this time, when they whooshed me, it took a little longer to get where we were going. It wasn't because this place was farther away, it was because they were preparing me for what was to come.

Before I go on with the rest of this story, there is something else I feel compelled to talk about. There's a question I'm sure each of us has asked ourselves at different times in our lives. For the past few days, it has been my main thought. You could look at me in a crowd and pass me right by. In a group of ten people, you could only see nine if I was included. I am an average, normal, even boring person that does not stand out in any way. So I could not get the question "Why me?" out of my mind.

I don't know about you, but when I ask that question, I pretty much do not expect an answer. I really do not consider myself special in any way. But lately, when I asked myself that question, what I witnessed would always come to me, and if it was not a direct answer, at least it satisfied my question.

What I'm about to tell ya would certainly qualify me as crazy, that is if you already haven't put me there. If not crazy, maybe someone on drugs. Be that as it may, I still have to tell ya.

I will not put a number to it, but I will say that there have been many, many people that I have seen in all my travels with Tick and Tock. Of all the people there I saw, it was never the same person twice. What kinda made me laugh were the different "personalities" that each person had with them. I'm sure I got a few snickers myself for being led around by Tick and Tock. Some people were being led by cell phones, some by animals, some by shoes, some even by, yea, you guessed it, even angels.

If I were to guess, I would guess that there are different levels of remembering. In all my years of traveling to many different times on the calendar, I have recognized people on the street from up there. Most have walked right by me without even a nod or a wink. Others looked at me and then looked again, as if tryin' to place where they saw me. Yet there was one person who I actually talked with comparing our experiences. It was a comfort to know I had a travelin' partner, of sorts.

Back to the question, "Why me?" Well, I had a sneakin' suspicion that everyone has taken a trip or two at some point in their life. So if we all have, then I guess that satisfies that question for me.

There is nothin' wrong in trying to prepare yourself for life. Doing research, investigating, askin' questions, and getting answers is a good thing. But sometimes, it doesn't really help at all. For example, you can read all the books on marriage and how to do it right, but all those books don't really help. It's just theory until both parties conquer their own wills. Knowin' about stuff is quiet different than knowin' "how" to do it.

Well, Tick told me that where we were going tonight was goin' to be way different than before. If I didn't know any better, I would say he was tryin' to scare me. He wasn't tryin' to scare me though, he was just tryin' to prepare me. I thought he did a pretty good job preparing, that was, until we reached our destination.

One of the first things I noticed was that so much of the original color was missin'. All that was left were the colors we are all familiar with today. Yet even these colors were missin' something. It was like all the life was removed from them.

Another thing I took note of, we weren't in The Garden anymore. The realization of it all was like gettin' kicked in the chest by a horse. I read about this happenin' in the Bible but to actually experience the before and after was a total shock to my system. No amount of preparedness could have prepared me for getting kicked out of The Garden.

We were all born in a corrupt and messed-up world. But that is our normal, we may not like it, but we are all used to it. But now that I got a taste of The Garden, I see how we were supposed to live and how beautiful our original home was. The fragrance of life in The Garden goes beyond words. But here, the smell of death infected even my thoughts.

I found Adam hidden behind a tree. Remember all those things that I told you hadn't been born yet? Fear, jealousy, greed…well, here in their infancy, they were as strong as ever. They were alive and well and as hungry and dangerous as a lion on the prowl.

Here in this place outside The Garden, Death was very much alive. There was no unity, no workin' together, and no colors that connected us. Intrinsic in the colors: joy, wisdom, love was a penetrating quality that worked in everything at The Garden. That quality was absent here. As a matter of fact, quite the opposite was true now.

The colors that we are familiar with today have a kind of virus woven in them with the intention to separate and antagonize. Taking it even a step further, if you can think of colors as words, then maybe you'll begin to understand. The words are joined together with a purpose. The words on this page are telling a story. Words form sentences that relay ideas, messages, and actions. There is a purpose for every word in a sentence. In The Garden, that purpose was done by a master artist with good intentions. Out here in this abyss, there is another artist at work with a different purpose. Not a good one either. Not a good one at all.

I wanted to leave here and go back, but to where? My own time and place? It didn't seem right for me there, now! I've tasted The Garden and the taste of life is in me now. Do you remember experiencing the colors with me in The Garden, how it was a total experience? Now, there is a different color here, and believe me, it is a total experience. If I had to put a name to it, it would be Death. I could see it, I could smell it, and I could even taste it. Everywhere I looked, everything was either dead or dying.

When we were in The Garden, Adam was the one who approached me. He was inviting and filled with Joy. Today, he would not come to me, I had to be led to him. To look at his appearance, he was no different. But his actions were that of a different person completely. Today, he looked like an angry little man. That scared me and I'll tell ya why in a minute.

Adam talked and I listened—again. What did I have to offer? Was my life perfect? Were all my choices right? Heck, as a matter of fact, all the people I cared the most about in my life I had driven away. So I knew how to mess up a life, but I had no idea how to restore one. So I listened.

Adam told me of the new things he's been experiencing. Sadness, pain, nakedness, cold…and so much more. Confusion was a big part of his life now. He communicated to me that the gravity of his situation was not realized when he was *told* about death, but only when death was performed right before my eyes. He was given some clothes, and as a result, some animals had to be put to death. Even some of the ones he named. He was repulsed by the act and all the blood. But he was comforted with the warmth of the covering. The shame of being naked was all but gone. Simply put, the same act, killing and skinning, brought both revulsion and comfort. Yea, Adam was confused as was I.

The main problem was not the problem itself, the problem was that we saw no solution at all. He was done, we were done, we were doomed. Was Adam gonna end skinned and be someone else's coat? Or worse than that, was I gonna have to witness that event? Oops, there I go thinkin' of myself again.

Now, back to why I was so disturbed by Adam and how he reacted. When I met Adam for the first time in The Garden, I met someone that I was meeting for the first time. What I mean by that is that Adam was unique unlike anyone I have ever met before. He was The Perfect Man, having qualities that were ideal but not attainable. He did not remind me of anyone and no one I ever met reminded me of him. Then when I met that angry little man behind that tree, he reminded me of just about everyone I've ever met. Takin' it even a step further, when I saw Adam, it was like I was lookin' in a mirror. I saw myself, and that is what scared me.

Adam was all alone. I don't mean that there weren't people around him. He had Eve and others around. The memory of The Garden was with him, the plants and animals, the way they were, and the One that gave him life were all in the past. There were still plants, animals, and even Eve, but the way it was now, was less. Adam was separated and alone.

It's one thing to live in ignorance and then it is another to know how things should be, but are not. I've read about places like the Grand Canyon or Niagara Falls, and thought how nice it must be to see them. But until you feel the power of the wind and water, all it is, is just a nice place. Well, I've read about The Garden in the Bible and always thought how nice it must have been. But now, all I can do is weep at its loss.

Before my visit to The Garden and meeting with Adam, my thoughts were that I had led a successful life. Lookin' from the outside, you would probably think so too. I had my retirement income that gave me more than enough to live on. My house and car were all paid in full. Isn't that what life is all about? Workin' until you retire and restin' until you die? Yea, that's what I thought too. When all you've known is a certain way of life, that way of life is normal to you. No matter how bad or good it is, it seems normal. If all you've known is either riches or pain, after a while, the only time it seems abnormal is when it is removed. My eyes have been opened to the way it should have been and so now I look at the mess I've made of *my own* life with new eyes.

But for now, I'm out of the past and back into the present. At this point, I'm layin' in my bed and I'm feelin' feelings and thinkin' thoughts that I've never been in touch with before. I'm feelin' lost like I've never felt lost before. I've read the Bible and I know that there's a Jesus and He died for your and my sin. I went through that process as a youngster. Yet now, I was as confused as ever. If I were to believe all that has happened in my nightly excursions, then the conclusion I come to is that in my present state, I'm at the mercy of my surroundings. I believe in heaven and that I'll end up there eventually, but for now, it seems I must suffer through this life. And knowing what I know now, it is only suffering that I have to look forward to.

There I was, tryin' to finish my cup of coffee and toast but only just touchin' it. I've never not finished my coffee, but this morning, I didn't have the gumption to empty my cup. It just didn't taste good this morning. I was on automatic pilot this morning, but even that seemed to be broken. The stuff I do without even thinkin' about went undone today. Checkin' the mail, waterin' the lawn, and even though I sat in front of the morning news, I don't remember a thing about it. It felt like I was broken.

It seemed that all the life had been sucked out of me and I didn't know how to put it back. I, of all people, did not know how to put life back into something that has died. My plan was to lie around, empty inside, and see if Tick and Tock would either fix this problem or take me away for good. That's how bad I felt. I was so dumbstruck that day that I remember walking right into a closed door. Bumped my nose and everything. If there was any pain, I didn't feel it.

I dreaded going to bed that night. If Tick and Tock didn't show up, I would be alone with my thoughts, and at the moment, that didn't sound so comforting. My mind kept going to three different places. The first place was the beauty and majesty of The Garden. But it didn't stay there, too bad. Because then, it would travel to the place where Adam seemed like a scared little man. My mind didn't stay there either, which is a good thing, but then it went to a time before I started my Garden treks, when I lived in ignorance. I almost miss my ignorance. But when you lose your ignorance, there is no way to get it back. Ya gotta laugh though, here I was thinkin all this—before I went to bed.

5

The Baby

I finally made it to bed. There I was, counting the seconds on the clock as if they were days. Then I heard my friend's voice. Tick asked me the same question that was asked after that first morning, "Are you still believing?" I have to admit that I was hesitant. But I said yes, and he said, "Come on then." I am so glad I said yes. Boy, did I get some good news!

First off, let me say this, there is so much that happens that we people do not have a clue about. There are some things that we people know and understand, at least to a certain degree. We know that we can't survive without water, we know that night follows day, and we know that pain hurts. There are other things that go way beyond our understanding and so we theorize (make stuff up) and then because it sounds good, we state it as fact. Let me tell you, truth is more real that fact.

At the beginning of this particular journey, we had to stop and eat 'cause Tick said I would need what this food provided. We were to have more than one place to go this morning. I was fed a little piece of bread and a cup of wine. There was something in that food that made me feel young again or, better yet, brand-new. I didn't exactly know what it was, but I knew what it wasn't. It wasn't drugs and it wasn't fake.

As I was renewed, I was led to a place that I guess you could call the middle of forever. There I was, in a barn where a baby had just been born. There were a few people coming to see someone amazing. But besides the people I saw, there was also a sound I heard that was out of this world.

The sound that I heard was a song. The (another) weird part was it was sung in a language I have never heard before, yet I understood every note and every word. The song that I heard was sung by a voice. But not the voice of one person. I will fall short tryin' to describe it, but I will try anyway. If you can imagine a hundred-person choir, then imagine a hundred of those choirs, all in perfect pitch and perfect time, so much so that they had just one sound. Again, in my heart, I knew that this sound did not come from anything of this world.

The beauty of the sound was not the thing that made my jaw drop in amazement. The song told a story and as it unfolded I was struck by a feelin' that I can only begin to describe. Ya know that feelin' you get when you're tryin' to remember something you forgot? And then you remember it! Or maybe you're tryin' to figure out a problem and the solution evades you, until—boom! And then you get it. There was something I had forgotten and there was a problem that needed figuring out, and this song addressed both of these situations with simplicity and clarity.

As the song unfolded, I studied this newborn baby and I began to notice something familiar about him. I didn't know what it was yet or where I remembered him from, I just know I had seen him before. And then it happened, it was like the lights coming on for the first time. When we looked at each other and our eyes locked on one another, we communicated, or I should say that he did, I just listened. I recognized what was so familiar. This infant reminded me of Adam. But as I came to understand, it wasn't that this newborn looked like Adam, it was the other way around, Adam looked like him. Even though this baby was brand-new in the world and Adam was way back in time, this infant was much, much older. This child not only reminded me of Adam, but also many other people that had been in my life. There were people that came to my mind that had the same look as this baby had. My pastor for one, also some of my teachers, neighbors, and friends. And then I heard his father name this amazing baby, he said, "His name shall be Jesus."

Gettin' Wet

Then I was whooshed away, Tick did some more talkin', and Tock did some more tickin'. We had left for another time. Now the child had grown to adulthood. The song continued, it seemed to be coming from everywhere and nowhere at the same time. Tick told me that it was coming from a place that he couldn't take me to yet, but it was a place very, very close. He said that everyone there was singin' and celebrating, that's why it sounded the way it did.

We had come from the stable and were now at a river. It seemed I was being led to places of beginnings. I went to Adam's beginning, Eve's beginning, Death's beginning, Jesus's birth, and now it looked like I was at some other type of beginning.

I saw a river with a line of people that went on as far as my eyes could see. There were men, women, children, and whole families waiting in this line. One man was in the front and they were all coming to him. He was in the water, each person would come to him, one at a time, and then he would say some words and then dunk them under the water. The closer I got, the clearer his words became. He appeared mad at a group of men, callin' them snakes. But as mad as he was, he turned no one down the opportunity to get wet. The people coming out of the water were weeping uncontrollably, but I could tell that every one of them seemed lighter on their feet and filled with Joy.

Then I saw him. The baby was all grown up. He came to the water and it was as though the water invited him in. The man who Jesus came to, his name was John. John wanted to trade places with Jesus, but Jesus's response was "Not today." Let me back up for a second. Each and every person that came to John told on themselves. Even the little ones told the bad things they had done. But when Jesus came to John, he had nothing to tell on himself about. He just told John to continue and dunk him.

All of a sudden, there was a shift. The song stopped as Jesus went into the water. As he came up out of the water, there was something like a door opening above him and a little bird came to him from that opening and they were joined. I remember my thought at the time was when that bird and Jesus locked eyes together, there was a look of recognition and welcome that passed between them. As this was happening, there was silence everywhere. Not a cricket sounded, not a bird chirped, and not a baby made a noise. Total silence, like I've never heard before. Then out of that opening in the sky, a voice spoke that was both familiar and ancient. The voice identified Jesus as his pleasing son. I will never forget that moment.

The moment faded even though the memory didn't. Tock moved us on to our next destination. The song continued to be sung as the excitement from the choir consumed the song. Think of it this way: consider a city that was poor or even bankrupt, and they had won a lottery that gifted them absolutely no more financial burdens or worries. They had even won enough money to help out other cities. Think of the joy and excitement of each and every resident of that city. Imagine the dancing and the songs they would sing. That's the kind of excitement that was coming from this choir. Actually, the excitement I was listening to would make that city's celebration seem dull and boring.

7
The Cross

As the singers sang, the story continued. The song slowed down and came to the place of betrayal and judgment. The place in history Tock took me to was full of pain and agony. We stopped at a place where we saw three men nailed to a cross. A few of the people around them were weeping, the rest of the people were laughing and mocking them. As I was watching this happen, it just didn't seem right, but the song made me to understand the necessity of how this was played out.

The man that was centered on the cross was the man I recognized as the man Jesus. The same Jesus I saw as a baby. The same Jesus I witnessed being baptized by a man named John. Now I was here to see this life end. As we locked eyes again, I heard him say, "It is finished."

Tock took me as Tick talked. All that was happenin' on this trip seemed to me to be a lot to take in on at once. I asked if we were done for now. Tick told me that it may be finished, but we weren't done yet. Tick went on to say that he was done, but I wasn't. He was gonna drop me off with a good friend of his to take over my journey.

I was let off on a road that seemed deserted and was told that a friend would be arriving soon to lead me on. I saw him coming from a distance. The closer he came to me did *not* help me get a clear picture of him. He seemed familiar, yet his face blended in with his surroundings, making his facial features vague and indistinct.

He talked, I listened. We were not introduced yet he addressed me by my full name, the name that was on my birth certificate; Walter Buzz Storys. I don't remember anyone ever callin' me by my full name. Yet it seemed perfectly natural coming from him. He captured my attention immediately.

He began tellin' me about all the things I had done in my life. This would have been all right with me, if he had stopped there. But for every thing he told me that I had done, he also added the reasons why. And believe me, that totally messed up even all the good things I had accomplished. There is not enough room to go into detail, but let me just say that all my motivations were bred from either fear, greed, pride, or a mixture of the three. And he was absolutely right in everything he said. I was terrified.

We continued walkin', and to my relief, he had changed the subject. Two more men came alongside us that were dressed in robes and sandals. They were downcast and talkin' about Jesus and his crucifixion. They said they were on their way to a town near Jerusalem. I may have only been a spectator here, but believe me, I spectated very well. I listened to every word.

The man I was with appeared to be ignorant of the events surrounding Jesus's crucifixion. The two men began to explain that the followers of this Jesus expected him to take his role as king and lead an army to save his people. But instead of taking his role as leader, he let himself be taken and killed. They said of all the things he was able to do, he could not save himself. It was clear that they felt betrayed and confused.

Then the man I was with began to talk about something that was written in a book, and this book was written a long, long time ago. There was something very interesting that happened as this man began to talk. The song had continued to play up until this man started talkin'. When the man started talkin', the song stopped. Yet even though the song stopped, the message of the song did not miss a beat, but continued on in the story the man was tellin'.

He said that this book, called the Bible, the one that they believed in, talks of a special person that describes this man Jesus perfectly. It not only describes what he looks like and does, but also where he came from and also his suffering. He said the Bible actually talks all about Him from cover to cover. He concluded by saying that it wasn't over yet.

The two men convinced the lone man to follow them into town to refresh himself and grab a bite to eat. As everyone waited for the food to be made ready, the conversation drifted to what was said by the friends of the two men. They said their friends were spreadin' rumors that Jesus was up and walkin' around. As they were talkin', the food came, the man blessed the food, and when he was done, his face became clear and we all recognized him to be Jesus.

When it was perfectly clear that this man was Jesus, he said one more thing and then disappeared from their sight. Disappeared, vanished, had been transported, however you want to put it, he had been supernaturally taken away from that table. Added to the fact that he was now alive and *not* dead, we could see that something special was going on here. Now, remember, I had come from a time of automobiles, airplanes, space travel, computers, microwave ovens, and the list goes on. Maybe we (mankind) can bring back a life, but only if they have been dead for moments. This Jesus had been dead for three days. He had bled out, then been buried. Now he was up, walkin' around and appearing to be brand-new. Then he does something not even our modern technology could come close to doing: disappearing right before our eyes. He wasn't under the table or behind a wall, drugs were not a part of this. But before he left, he said those two little words that I have been hearing since this journey began: "Just believe!"

I came to myself in my own living room, yet this journey was still happening. The song that I heard playin' had started playin' again as soon as Jesus vanished. That was one of the reasons I knew I was still "in transport." I'm listenin' to the song and just waitin', then, all of a sudden, I hear a knock at my front door. I remember thinkin' that this was my house, I bought it, I paid for it, I own it, so why was I hesitant to answer my own front door? I heard the knock again, a little fainter this time. I knew I needed to get up and answer the door, and so I did. When I opened the door, there he stood, Jesus, the one I've been seeing throughout the course of my wanderings. He was the perfect gentleman. His words were, "May I come in?"

This time, without hesitation, I opened the door and he came right in. We went to the kitchen table and we both sat down. I remembered my manners and asked if I could get him something to eat or drink. He responded that coffee sounded pretty good. I walked over to the coffee pot to get it ready, but the pot had just finished percolating. If anybody asks how Jesus takes his coffee, you can tell 'em that he takes it black. Actually, we both did. I don't know about you, but I found this experience quite odd. Here I was sitting in my kitchen with this person who…?

He gave me time with my thoughts before he addressed me. We both sipped our coffee, enjoying its flavor. My thoughts went to "Who exactly was this sittin' at my table?" I was told before all this began about a "Jesus," but to be honest, I thought "Jesus" was just a religion like all the others and going to church was something good people do. I never considered for an instant that "Jesus" was a real person, or that all the stories in the Bible were true. Guess what? He is and they are!

The song continued to be sung. Again, I could not tell exactly where it was coming from other than somewhere outside. Everything was perfectly real, cars were driving by, I heard kids playin' in the street, I even heard a siren in the distance. Then I heard Jesus ask me the million-dollar question, "Do you know who I am?" I could not look him in the eyes as I told him, "I thought so." He asked me again, "Do you know who I am?" This time I answered with a big fat "Yes." He responded, "Who do you say I am?" His eyes were penetrating to my soul. His words touched my heart like nothing else ever has. His words and his gaze told of a love that went way beyond anything human. I answered back what I knew to be true. I answered back what the song continued to sing about. I answered back that I knew he was the Son of God. I told him that I knew he came on this earth as a babe and that he grew up specifically to die on the cross for me. And I told him I knew that he is still alive today. I concluded by saying how much of a jerk I was, how much I messed up everyone's life around me, and that I was sorry for doing it and for not seeing all this before. We both started cryin' happy tears, and he said that he would help me with everything. Then all of a sudden, the most amazing thing happened. The song that was playin', it faded. I could no longer hear it with my ears. Now, it was on the inside and I could hear it with my heart.

Many things happened next, and many more things did not happen next. I came to myself in my bed. I was fully refreshed and feelin' like new. It was faint, but I could still hear the song deep inside my heart. It continued to be sung. Tick and Tock would be back, this I knew, but it would not be for a while. The purpose of my nightly adventures ended over coffee with my new friend. Now, there would be another beginning of sorts.

I went to the kitchen for more coffee and some toast. A new thought came to me as I was sippin' my coffee. I went to the bookshelf, wiped the dust off of my old Bible, and sat down with it. Ya know, this may have been just me, but I could have sworn that as I sat down the clock in my kitchen smiled at me.

Epilogue
Not the End

Well, you might say that the previous chapter would be a great place to end this tale, but you would be wrong. That would only be half the story. So far, this story is exciting and entertaining, but if it ended there, I probably would have not told anyone about what happened to me. I would have hidden it in my heart and cherished it privately. But because of what happened next, I feel a need to make sure ya'll get the whole story.

To do that, I'm going to invite someone else to complete this story with us. First, let me tell you of how this is gonna work. I'm gonna tell ya a little bit about the kinda person I was before all this happened. After that, someone else is gonna come and tell ya their version of who I used to be and who I am today.

Earlier in this story, I may have made it sound like I was a happy camper and had it all together. Well, nothing could be further from the truth. My main issue was that I owned a house that was way to big for me. I guess I'm gonna have to explain that. Ya see, I live in this big ole house alone. The people that cared the most for me I had driven away. I told myself almost every night that they were wrong and it was all their fault. I think deep down in my heart, I knew better, I just couldn't admit it to myself.

What do you do with someone who is always right and has to prove it loudly and with long arguments? Of course, I was not always right, and when this happened, I had to prove it more vigorously. Would you like to live with this person? Well, my wife put up with me and my ways until our children were all grown up. After that, she left and moved in with someone else, my sister of all people! We didn't get a divorce or anything, we just parted company.

Even though I loved her, I told her good riddance because, of course, "I was right." This was where I was trapped in my pride, which said the most important thing was for me to be "right." If she couldn't live with it, then it was better for her to go. Yet it still broke my heart. She called every now and then to see how I was doing, but our conversations were with short sentences and small words. I still loved her and so I wondered when she was going to change and come back to me. Lookin' back, I really surprise myself in my stupidity and arrogance.

It was the same with my children too. I demanded perfection from them. Of course, they weren't perfect, so they suffered the consequences. Now, as a result of my imperfections, sometimes, I got a call during the Christmas holidays from them. I had never seen my grandkids up to that point. They said that they did not want to subject their babies to my way of life. At the time, I thought, "Oh well, their loss." I could not even admit at the time that my heart was breaking. So my house and I stayed to ourselves. I knew my house would never leave me. Also, my house always did what I asked of it. Now tell me, did I seem all right to you?

That was the kinda person I was and that's how I remained—until my encounter with Jesus. Something happened in me that began to change how I thought about people and how I thought about myself.

But enough of my talk now, let me introduce you to my lovely wife, Joyce.

Joy Talks

As Wally (my pet name for him), told you, my name is Joyce, but most people call me Joy. There is a whole lot to tell, and right now, I'm wondering exactly where to start.

Let me begin by telling you a little about myself. Wally and I are the same age. I am a retired schoolteacher who taught grades first through sixth. I have always loved children, which is why I went into teaching. I simply love being a part of learning.

I started walking with Jesus as a teenager and never stopped. When I met Wally at the age of twenty, Jesus told me that he was the one I was to marry. I never expected marriage to be easy, but I also never expected it to be as difficult as it was. But as hard as it was, I can say today that it was worth it.

Wally grew up to be an angry little man. He did not start out that way, but that was the way he was when God finally touched him. According to Wally, there was only one way to do anything: that was his way. Any other way than his and you would see a little kid tantrum coming from an adult. It was not a pretty sight. There were times when he would come home for lunch and see our children's chores undone. Guess what he would do? He would go to their school, make a fuss, drag them home for them to complete their chores correctly. That was his way. Was it any wonder they maintained their distance from him when they became old enough to make their own decisions?

He was the same way with me also. If he did not like the way dinner was prepared, he would throw it in the trash. That happened more times than can be counted. I would always tell our children not to give up hope, that God can change Wally's heart. To tell the truth, I had to encourage myself with those very same words. When our children grew up, they moved out and did not look back.

After they moved out, I was right behind them. I believe our kids lost hope for Wally, but I did not. I stayed in contact by phone. Every so often, I would call to check on him, but clearly, there was no evidence of any change in him.

Until, one day, I received a phone call from Wally. This "Wally" was a Wally that was brand-new to me. All I could make out over his weeping was that he was sorry. Two things I have never heard from Wally was the word "sorry" or heard him shed any tears. This Wally was a different person. As Wally was crying to me, I heard God tell me to go to my husband.

I left right away. It was about an hour's drive to get there from where I was staying. When I had finally arrived, I was weeping too. There was much God had told me during the drive "home." He did not tell me the particulars of Wally's transformation, but what he did tell me was to believe all my new husband would tell me. His exact words to me were "just believe."

If I was excited when I arrived home, Wally was like electricity times two. He was crying and laughing at the same time. By the time I had pulled into the driveway and exited the car, he was out of our home and had me in his arms. He almost carried me into our home just like he did the first time.

We sat down at our kitchen table across from each other. He then proceeded to beg my forgiveness for the way he was in our past. He was very specific. As he brought up these past events, the memory of them brought back the pain almost like it was happening again. It was almost more than I could bear. The abuse to the children, to me, the yelling, the embarrassment, the separation, the coldness toward us...all the pain came back and hit me all at once. I finally asked him to stop, and he did! That alone was surprising.

He let me calm down quietly and then he told me the most incredible story. It was no different then the story told here on these pages. His excitement was contagious. As he was telling me what had happened and where he had gone, we walked around the block, sat in the backyard, he even cooked us dinner.

One thing I neglected to say earlier was that when I drove up to the house, something seemed different. Nothing I could really point a finger at to say precisely, "That's different." Just that things were not quite the same as when I left. The children in the neighborhood smiled at us. The neighbor's cat strolled across our lawn and Wally let it pass. Inside the house, things were clean but not shiny. I liked it. And finally, our neighbor's dog came though a doggy door that was built in our fence. Apparently, this was all Wally's doing. I changed my mind, I did not like it, I loved it! This was truly a new Wally.

We sat and talked all through the night and into the next day. He was actually changing right before my eyes. He would get up to rewash the dishes, catch himself in the act, come back and sit down, giving me a sheepish smile and a shrug. Without saying a word to each other, his actions spoke volumes to us. That's what I felt different when I drove up to our house, someone vastly different was housed in it!

I do not know what to call it. Maybe it is a lack of faith on my part? Or maybe it's that when God steps in and does something, it is unbelievable. I have seen God do some amazing things in my lifetime, but not to someone so close to me or in this fashion. I would not have been very surprised if Wally had unzipped his skin and somebody else popped out. Believe me, I looked for the zipper!

So the point that I would like to focus on is not just what God has done for Wally, but also how it affected his life. The old Wally and the new Wally are two totally separate people. Is Wally perfect? Not by a long shot. He is still changing today. Just to keep things in perspective, I'm still working on me too. Wally and I are back together, our neighborhood has taken on a new personality, our children are back in Wally's life, and now even our grandchildren have a grandfather who was not available before. The list of changes goes on. The list of people affected by Wally's transformation if you were to put a number on it could very well be in the hundreds or even the thousands.

Well, I believe I've said enough for now. It was truly my pleasure to do my part in telling you about Wally. So I will say good-bye for now and give you back to Wally. But before I go, I would like to leave you with two little words that have had a great impact on both of our lives: "Just believe!"

Hey ya'll, it's me again, Walter. Believe it or not, everything Joy told ya was the truth. I didn't want to tell ya myself 'cause it would have seemed like braggin' to me. I just ain't really comfortable with braggin', so I let my wife do it for me. To me, it don't really seem like braggin' if someone else is doin' it for ya.

It's getting close time to sayin' good-bye for now. Don't worry though, Tock is still tickin' and Tick is still talkin', so I'll be getting back with ya'll shortly. Can I tell ya something a little bit weird before we part company? Even though we've never met or said hello, I feel pretty close to ya'll. So close in fact that if we ever met somewhere and ya came up to shake my hand, I would feel like I already know ya. But who knows, maybe we have met somewhere else!

So good-bye for now, with two final words given to me, I leave with you: "Just believe!"